Chapter One

Estimate

It was a lazy fall day as she sat and organized her paper work for tomorrow. She gazed at her husband sleeping in the chair wondering what else she could possibly to do keep herself from dying of complete boredom. A few hours later she got dinner started and on the table. Nice to see something wakes him from the dead as she thought to herself with a smile on her face as she served him his meal.

That night they got settled in and decided to watch a movie. She went onto check her emails to see if there were any new clients sent to her to follow up on. About two years ago she started her own cleaning company. It seemed to be booming for such a small town. About the time she was getting ready to close things up for the night the phone rang. She answered, "Thank you for calling Ghost Cleaners this is Mandy speaking how can I help you." She saw the name on the caller id and almost didn't answer the phone. What would be the odds of two people with that same name first and last calling from long distance number. She let Brian carry on for a while telling her what he was looking for. He was wanting an estimate for a farm house that needed to be cleaned. They talked for a bit and decided to meet up the next time he was in town so she could see the size of the house and what needed to be done with out being blind sighted. He got with her on dates and before they ended their conversation she had to ask if he by chance went to St. Vincent's which was their high school from way back when. She knew he was going to say yes because she remembered his voice like it was yesterday when she first said hi to him on the bus. After that she was hooked on hearing his voice. Not necessarily him, but his voice. She never quiet understood it. He threw a fit over the phone. "How the hell do you remember me just by riding the bus together that many years ago? She grinned and lied her ass off saying she didn't quiet remember just happened to recognize the name. She couldn't really say why with her husband sitting next to her in the chair even though he seemed oblivious to everything. They got off the phone laughing at each other and as she heard him say when he'd be home her heart skipped a major beat and the butterflies started fluttering. She was 17 all over again.

Chapter2

Train Tracks

It would be a few weeks before she saw him. The day finally came for their "reunion" as she called it. She basically lost a whole night's sleep and was so nervous she must have tried on 20 different outfits before saying to herself in the mirror" What are you doing stupid girl? You're married and you're as giddy as a school girl. Get over it. She decided on a pair of jeans and a long-sleeved t-shirt with a hoodie. It was fall so it was chilly out. That being said she gathered her books and office equipment and headed out to the country. It was a beautiful drive. Nothing but cornfields and butterflies for miles. Of course, she gets stopped by a train at the tracks. She decided to text him and let him know she was going to be a few minutes late no thanks to a train that had stopped her. As she was sitting at the tracks, she turned the radio up ironically "Just one look" was on which made her laugh. It started to get warm quick so she took her jacket off as she was doing so, she noticed a white truck pull up behind her and a man getting out the car. She panicked not knowing what to do. So, with her heart thumping she finished taking her jacket off the rest of the way and as soon as she did, he appeared beside her window saying "Take it off baby" (with a mischievous grin and that gleam in his eye) She knew right away it was him and her face turned beat red. First time ever she'd been speechless. Stopped at the tracks with the possible future love of her life this was to good to be true. All she could do was shake her head and get out of the car and talk to him wondering what the cars behind them were thinking. They gave each other hug and eventually the train cleared and they moved on to the farm house. It would be after that that many more weird moments like that would soon come.

Next day she showed up with her crew and he was impressed. Said that we were the only ones who actually showed up to work. We spent a majority of the day cleaning the house. It was a little difficult considering we had to get our water through a hose at the neighbor's house and carry it in by buckets to clean. The job was incredibly challenging to say the least. It took about a week or so to get that house in shape and she stayed with him until it was complete. In the process of finishing the

4

last of her chores upstairs she had over heard his conversation he was having with someone as she unplugged the vacuumed. He had joked with her earlier in the week about wearing a maid uniform and she not thinking anything of it rolled her eyes and went on about her day, but this was her perfect opportunity to get him. So right when she heard him say "No they don't wear those here" she knew exactly what they were discussing and yelled out over the stairs "We charge an extra $20.00 an hour to wear the outfits! (with a big grin)" She thought he was going to lose it all she heard him say was "Jesus" his face was red. Oh she got him good. She finished up and he was still rambling on about that subject. All she could do was shake her head pack up the car and leave. The next day they met up at the old farm house alone and he still wouldn't let up about the maid outfit. So, after he had paid her and they left and went their separate ways it wouldn't be until that January that he would receive a birthday card in the mail with a picture of her that her husband took just to get his goat. Oh, my goodness she got a phone call as soon as he got it. Right when she answers the phone she hears "Ya sick freak!" and they both laughed their rears off. After that it was the very beginning of a very interesting and unique friendship.

At that particular time frame, she was still married and he was dating someone, but not dating someone. From what she had gathered they had broken up over something and he was just back home thinking things through she had her friend with her she was ok with that.

SUMMER 2005

Country Wedding

That summer he called her to tell her that he had gotten married and would be coming home to have a second wedding in the country for family and friends back home. Her heart sank. She went to the wedding and he had left his ring somewhere so her husband had a ring for him to borrow for the ceremony. So once again when he put it one, he flipped because it was the same ring that he had. She sat there trying to figure them out she didn't feel the closeness like so many other weddings that she'd been to. She went through the motions and talked to his bride

Cashandra. She picked on her about little Brian's running

around. She said she couldn't wait for that to happen.

Gulf Shores, Alabama

2006

That summer Mandy decided to take a vacation to see her favorite performer sing. She called her friends in Alabama and set it up. She was surprised they let her stay with them being newly married and all. She didn't think much of it once she got down there. He was her home she was so used to dealing with him in person It was almost as if Cashandra didn't even exist. They got along well of course, but he was her world no matter what. Her and Cashandra had went out shopping to get ready for the big event. They came back drenched. The look on his face was priceless and he blurts out "Wet T-shirt contest!" It was a major monsoon outside. Of course, their monsoon season would last a whole ten minutes and they would be off to the show.

Jerry did an excellent job of keeping it a secret from Blair that Mandy would be there. So, she put a note on the piano with a song request and signed her name to it. She rejoined her friends and hid in the crowd. As he was going through the requests, he saw her. He stopped for a minute and grinned ear to ear. Across the microphone he called out "Now there's only one Mandy I know from Illinois if this is you please stand up and wave." She grinned and waved and ran up and gave him a huge hug.

They stayed and danced for hours on end. It came time for her friends to leave. Brian had offered to come back and pick her up after the show. Later that night she went back to their place and they had made plans to travel to a beach on the gulf that she hadn't seen yet. She finally fell into a peaceful sleep something had woken her up. Their cats were laying right beside her and one had just fallen off the bed backwards. So, at three o'clock in the morning she was in the worst laughing fit ever. Lord only knows what they were thinking about her.

The next day her and Brian took the ferry into the bay and spent time on the beach across the way. The day was absolutely amazing. She got to walk the beach with her friend. If someone would have told her in high school that she'd be doing this she wouldn't have believed them. She told her friend Blair he was going to get her in a heap load of trouble if he kept coming down to Alabama like this

He had a few phone calls to make and she found herself sitting peacefully on the beach with out a care in the world. He took a few photos of her and they continued their walk for a little while. They got back to the house and as they walked through the kitchen, he looks at her funny. She was like what? Didn't you have your wallet in your jean pocket? Oh no. All the money was completely soaked. So, they put the money out on the table to dry laughing as they did it. He's a bad influence on her she forgets about everything. She was really bummed that her sand dollar she had found had broken as well. He offered her one of theirs but she declined it just wasn't the same.

The next day she flew out and went home to Illinois having had the time of her life or so she had thought.

That winter he had planned a visit home and she had made it her life's mission to find his best friend for him. There was this social media thing online called Facebook she signed herself up on. Strangely enough she found him. They started talking and hanging out. She got along with his wife really well and met his whole family. It was like they never stopped talking.

When Brian and Cashandra flew home they planned a dinner that night and had his friend Evan there with her and his family. She had him facing the window to where he couldn't see them. They hadn't seen each other since they graduated high school which would have made it a 20-year mark or so. She greeted Brian and Cashandra when they got there. She had him look around the room to see if he recognized anyone so finally, she grabbed Evans elbow to turn around. Oh my gosh the joy on his face. They hugged each other so many times I found myself telling them to get a room. We all laughed. Brian's wife thought it was creepy how everyone knew each other. That told me all I needed to know about that right there. It was so busy we all decided to go to a Mexican restaurant to eat and we were so lost in talking we didn't even realize that the restaurant was closing. There was one moment at dinner as he was sitting his wife Cashandra down he looked at her and made a comment that even now she can't remember what he said, but couldn't believe that he had said it in front of her and had gotten really stand offish about the whole thing. Something told her something wasn't right if he was flirting with his wife around.

11

It would be that fall that he would call to tell her that his wife left him for another man. She was actually truly shocked. She thought they were pretty solid. Although the one conversation she'd had with his wife that prior summer about an ex of hers. Well let's just say that if I were to have been the newly married one to him, I'd be bragging about him something awful not my ex. That's another story for another time. But in the meantime, he's telling her all of this and the best advice she could give him was to come home and get into a house project of some sort. He flew home and they got together the next night. They were sitting in her living room and something he said that even now she couldn't remember she just remembered his eyes staring right through her soul like rescue me. The only thing she could to was take him shopping. It's the best cure for depression and in the store, he looks at her and says you know you're right it does help. I'm a girl I know these things. They came back to the apartment and he gave her a hug good bye and said good night. The next day they met up to just roam through the countryside while he yelled at his ex-wife in the car with the music turned up loud. She just let him vent. The rest of his trip home was a blur to her she wanted to spend every single second she could be allowed with him. It was good for him to be home and bury some memories. It would be a few months before they spoke again, but he would ground her when he did call to her core.

THE DREAM

"Red Bar"

Her phone rang around midnight and totally freaked her out thinking someone was hurt or needed her. Quickly she answered the phone thinking omg, but it was his voice on the other line. Mostly mindless chitter chatter about their day what was new what wasn't what happened with the ex. Then he got really quiet and she asked him if he was ok. Quiet was not necessarily his thing. So, he says I had this dream about you and it didn't make any sense. So calmly with a huge smile on her face she was trying to hide she says well spill it. He was a little hesitating, but slowly started spilling the details. She watched her breathing she didn't want him to hear her silently freaking out.

They were in this club and there was a bar off to the side where they had gone in to get a drink and relax after an evening of dancing, but the floor and the bar itself had changed and so had I. I had on a black leather dress which was not me at all my hair was done differently. At one point he had sat his drink down and spread me across the bar hand cuffing my hands to the chains on the end.

14

With the music pumping in the back ground no one was paying attention as he grabbed ahold of her and held her from behind and slowly removing her panties as he undid his zipper to his goth outfit spread her legs apart taking every inch of her in. Teasing her with the cherry from his drink with the salty and the sweet. They were doing the kinky Calypso dance. The part that didn't make any sense at all was once he was through satisfying their every single need in front of everyone there was a line of guys at the door, he handed them all condoms and said have fun as he walked away. She couldn't help but laugh on the last part. She decided to take the analytical route and said well it's probably because you're stressed and since I've been the one constant it's only natural for you to have a dream. Our bodies handle stress differently. They talked themselves to sleep then she decided to go down to visit that Valentine's weekend. What she didn't know was that her favorite band would be down there playing. That just added to the sweetness of it.

Fight or Flight

Valentines weekend had arrived back on the plane again to Alabama. She threw her ear buds in during take off and turned on Jason Mraz's song "I'm yours" closed her eyes and just grinned ear to ear. Thinking of the dream he told her about excited to see her favorite guys playing for Valentines day. She was truly in heaven. Before she knew I the plane touched down and she had arrived. He was waiting for her at the airport. She would stay with him that weekend. The house had a weird feel to it. There was this one chair in the kitchen she was drawn to, but couldn't understand why. The whole place smelled of his cologne. It was like it had put her in an instant trance. He had a few calls to make so as he was making calls, she was sitting on the floor unpacking her stuff. There was a particular outfit that she came across and couldn't help but smile, but apparently smiled to long. When he was done with the phone call, he called her on it. Turning around with those blue eyes of steel asking "What was that big smile about?" I said absolutely nothing and smiled. Ok so when he was married it was easier to give him hell about things. Now that he's single, she felt like she was the shy girl back in high school again. He was wearing her favorite grey sweater that really brought out the blue in his eyes and as she was watching him while still sitting on the floor, he walks up to his bedroom door opens it with his left arm and stands there and smirks. That smirk. She knew she was in trouble, but figured he was going to say it anyway.

So, about that dream? Her face went 60,000 shades of red. He told her more in detail about it and she couldn't do anything. So, when he asked her what she thought all she could say was she needed to go shopping. He was like seriously? So, he took her to the store and she went into Walgreens wanting to be prepared for anything that may happen. The week went on. The next day she went to the gulfarium to meet a dolphin. It was extremely chilly out, but she didn't care at all. (Cue Train "Soul Sister) The dolphins were dancing.

She got back to the house and waited for him to get off work. Taking in every single smell and texture. Ended up falling asleep on the couch. He startled her when he walked through the door. That night they went out to dinner. It was a waterfront restaurant that she had never been to, but the food wasn't bad. They talked, but it seemed like he was elsewhere. It turned out to be a night of nothing. Eventually she started getting ready for bed and gathered her books to start her homework. He was sitting at the computer checking up on work emails that night. She got all warm and cozy in bed as her bed was on the fold out couch in the "office" She got lost in studying and was mumbling about something she didn't get when he spun around in his chair looking extremely tired. He put his hand on his neck and had that smirk again that made his blue eyes sparkle deviously. He started to talk about the dream again and I said well why don't we go to the castle and re-live it? She wanted to see the room and experience everything. Then he asked her about oral sex. She blushed and said that she was flattered, but she was married. Strangely enough he said he'd forgotten that she was. That next night they would go to the club and dance. Even though present day this happened many years ago the thoughts of this night still make her blush.

That day they went shopping for a club outfit. Being a country girl, she had nothing of the sort and never really gave it a thought. She was comfortable in blue jeans, bare feat and a comfortable shirt. They walked through a few stores as he searched through the clothes. She had commented that this all felt weird to her having her guy friend pick out an outfit for her to wear. Usually it was one of her family members that would do that. So, as he picked out some outfits, she blushed big time when he held a red corset up with a short skirt. She thought if she'd bent over that night everyone would see everything. She went to the dressing room and tried them on laughing at herself. She picked the corset and the skirt. She had to admit he had great taste in clothing. It was then he looked at her and said, "Remember I was married once" She at that very moment had realized that even she forgot he had been because he sure wasn't acting like it that night.

As she was getting ready that night and putting her make up on, she suddenly remembered the night that got her into trouble about all of this, but it never came to mind until now though she had a funny feeling when he stopped dead in his tracks on the street that night and just stared at her. She was with her two best guy friends and they were telling stories of old and she told her one about when she got her dentures at a young age and how the guys used to pick on her. Oh boy did they run with that one, but it was at that moment she knew the way he looked at her. That bundle of nerves in the pit of her stomach as if she were to make a speech for the first time in front of everyone. Her thoughts were interrupted by his knock asking if she was ready yet. She was she just got carried away with old thoughts from their earlier days. Is this all that he's thought about since that night with out telling her directly, because he's as shy as she is?

They walked out the door and got in the car to head off to the club. He had his cologne on and she was mesmerized by it. She wanted to ask what kind it was, but was to timid. Half an hour later they got to the club. They were playing 80's techno music. Immediately she perked up and forgot all about feeling half naked in the outfit. A place she blended in well. Most of the guys there were gay and some drag queens she felt completely comfortable and not alone at all. They had agreed it was a non-date so she could roam wherever the mood struck mostly staying with the 80's music. He found the hottest stripper and took a photo with her and she thought she found a hot guy he walked all over the club with a long black vampire coat on and had the long hair and deep dark eyes she was always attracted to. Brian took a photo of them together since she thought he was cute and named him Nick. She laughed. When the music started to slow, he took her on a tour of the club. When they made it upstairs, he said this is it this is the room. She stopped dead in her tracks. They went in the room and there was the feeling in the pit of her stomach again. The bar was to the right as he said and the tables and lounge couches were on the left. Suddenly she felt completely naked. Then as if he read her mind he had asked if she was ready to leave as it was getting to be around 1am. She agreed it was freezing outside so she stole his jacket from the car. They drove back to his place in complete silence with some type of random music on in the car. They got in the house not knowing much of what to do she went into the bathroom and cleaned up a little bit. He had gone to the back room to turn the computer on and she went to warm up with blankets. He had checked his email she couldn't handle the silence so she got up to get something to drink. He follows her into the kitchen crunching an ice cube then walks by her again then asks out of the blue. Last chance do you want to? Her mouth dropped open. Even after she had told him she was married he wanted to be bad. He kept walking in and out of the kitchen with a grin on his face like he knew she was going to cave at any minute. He eventually went in to check his emails one last time and kind of gave her a final last chance comment in which she became deathly silent. She couldn't think this was it this is what she had been waiting for forever. All she could hear was hearts song in her head "How do I get you alone" she had him alone and though she was married she figured this was her only shot. As he was turning off the computer, she silently said ok. He responded......Now? Well we can wait until tomorrow night if you like. He said no just give me a few minutes. So, she sat patiently on her bed trying to figure out what he could possibly be doing for that length of time. I mean she figured one thing obviously, but not what he had instore for her. Within a few minutes he came into her room to retrieve her. He put a chain around her neck and led her into his bedroom. It had wooden floors a queen-sized bed with mosquito drapes around it giving it the soft look. He had all dark maybe cherry wood dressers and a hope chest that at one point during the day had a nice collection of hats. The room had his smell of her favorite cologne in the room. He had candles lit and some type of crazy techno music on that kind of surprised her from the songs he did share with her were just a little different. The chair that she was drawn to was in the room and started making sense of her original thought. The chair was for her to sit and get comfortable while he chained himself to the ceiling. Getting that she was the dom in this situation she got right to it. She figured she may as well make him loose his breath in an instant. Her knees fell to the ground and she went to town on him. Tasting every single inch of his man hood placing one hand on his leg to steady herself she still wasn't sure of her limits on touching him so she kept it to a minimal. He wasn't one that seemed to like all of the cuddly, touching feeling stuff. She took a break for a second and decided to switch positions. She wanted to be like she was in the dream so he leaned her over the bed and spread her arms out gently caressing her arms sent chills down her spine. She thought this is it there's nothing stopping them. She had waited years for this. Their bodies became one and she gave him full permission to lift her skirt and as she did his head was near hers and he whispered "so you can feel skin on skin" she breathlessly whispered "Yes" when she gave him full permission to go as far as he wanted to he abruptly stopped dressed her back up and dressed himself back up and looked her deep in her soul and said "I can't I won't use you that way" It was 3am by this time and she was absolutely dazed and confused happy that they got this close, but shocked he pulled this on her. Maybe it was to soon maybe he was right and in time she would see that he was right it would be too soon.

CPSIA information can be obtained
at www.ICGtesting.com
Printed in the USA
BVHW032348030319
541685BV00001B/167/P

9 781797 673783